DISNEY · PIXAR

W9-CFE-229

Illustrated by the Disney Storybook Artists
Adapted by Caleb Burroughs

Published by Louis Weber, C.E.O., Publications International, Ltd.
7373 North Cicero Avenue, Lincolnwood, Illinois 60712
Ground Floor, 59 Gloucester Place, London W1U 8JJ

Customer Service: 1-800-594-8484 or customer_service@pilbooks.com

www.pilbooks.com

p i kids is a registered trademark of Publications International, Ltd.

Manufactured in China.

8 7 6 5 4 3 2 1

ISBN-13: 978-1-4127-9603-3
ISBN-10: 1-4127-9603-2

It was Nemo's first day of school!
"Hurry up, Dad!" the little clown fish called.
He was excited and did not want to be late.

Marlin was Nemo's dad. He was very protective
of his only son, who was still very young, and had
one fin that was smaller than the other.

The two fish got to school. "Be safe," said Nemo's dad. Nemo swam to meet all of his new friends.

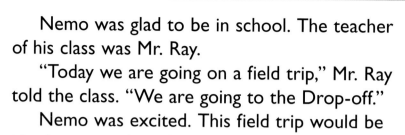

Nemo was glad to be in school. The teacher of his class was Mr. Ray.

"Today we are going on a field trip," Mr. Ray told the class. "We are going to the Drop-off."

Nemo was excited. This field trip would be his chance to show his new friends that he was brave. Forgetting his father's warnings, Nemo decided to show off.

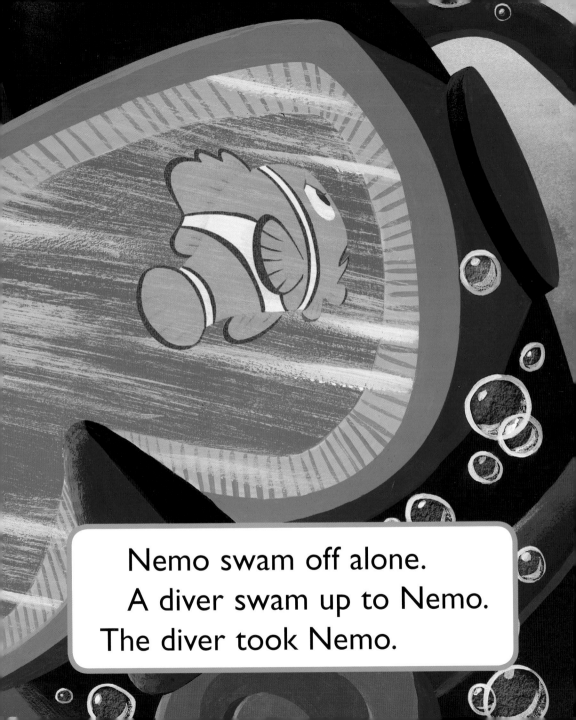

Nemo swam off alone.
A diver swam up to Nemo.
The diver took Nemo.

Learning that his son had been taken away, Marlin was worried. He had to find Nemo!

A friendly blue fish named Dory offered to help Marlin find his son. Even though Dory had trouble remembering things, she came along with Marlin.

They met three sharks. Then they found a mask. The mask was a clue!

Meanwhile, Nemo found himself someplace new and strange. The diver who caught him was a dentist. Nemo had been placed in an aquarium full of other fish which sat in the dentist's office.

Nemo soon befriended the other fish, named Bubbles, Jacques, Bloat, Gurgle, and Gill. A pelican named Nigel stopped by, too.

Soon Nemo learned some bad news. He was a gift for the dentist's niece, Darla.

Out in the middle of the ocean, Marlin and Dory met some very strange creatures. These fish were unlike anything they had ever seen.

One of the fish even had a light at the end of its antenna. "Let's use this light to read the mask we found," Dory suggested.

The two fish used the light
to read the mask.
    The mask told them that
Nemo was in Sydney!

As they tried to get to Sydney, Marlin and Dory ran into even more strange ocean creatures. But these creatures were dangerous. They were jellyfish, and their stingers were poisonous!

Marlin knew that jellyfish could hurt them. But he didn't want to scare Dory, so he turned it into a game of getting away from the jellyfish. But the two did not get away.

Dory was stung. She was sore and tired. Would they ever find Nemo?

Back in the aquarium, Nemo and his new friends had come up with a plan. The plan would allow him to escape before Darla, the dentist's naughty niece, took him away forever.

Nemo's job was to put a pebble in the tank's filter. When the water got dirty, the fish would be removed — and escape!

But the fish's plan did not work. Nemo did not escape.

Meanwhile, trying to find their way to Nemo, Marlin and Dory met a group of sea turtles.

Marlin told his problems to Crush, a very cool turtle.

Crush agreed to help the two fish on their quest to find Nemo.

Just when things were looking bad, they got worse. The dentist's niece Darla arrived at the office. The dentist put Nemo in a bag, to give to Darla as a gift. Nemo escaped from the bag.

When Marlin and Dory arrived in Sydney, they could not find Nemo. Marlin felt sad, sure that he had lost his son.

But Nemo had escaped—and soon Dory found him! Off the fish swam, happy to be back together once again.